First American Edition 2003
by Kane/Miller Book Publishers, Inc.
La Jolla, California

First published in Taiwan in 2001 under the title
"On My Way to Buy Eggs"
by Hsin Yi Publications, Taipei, Taiwan, R.O.C.

English translation published by arrangement with Hsin Yi Publications

 For information contact:
Kane/Miller Book Publishers
P.O. Box 8515
La Jolla, CA 92038
www.kanemiller.com

Library of Congress Control Number: 2002117381

Printed and bound in Singapore

1 2 3 4 5 6 7 8 9 10

ISBN 1-929132-49-2

On My Way to Buy Eggs

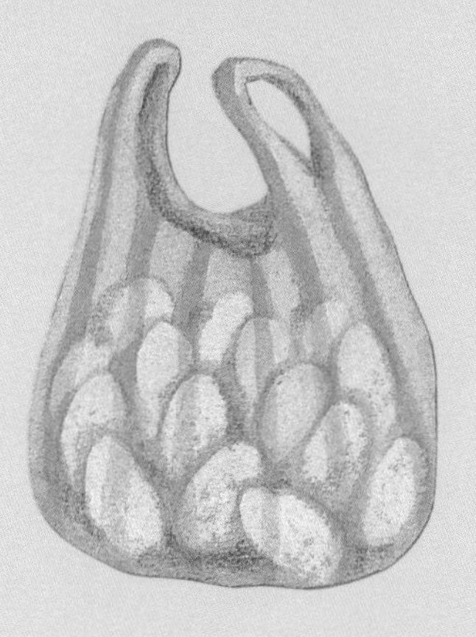

Written and illustrated by

Chih-Yuan Chen

Kane/Miller

BOOK PUBLISHERS

"May I go outside and play?" Shau-yu asks.

"I need you to go to the store first," her father replies. "We're out of eggs."

Shau-yu puts the money in the right pocket of her skirt.
(There are no holes in that pocket.)

Outside, she follows the cat's shadow. He's walking on the roof.

She peeks around the wall. "Woof, woof," she barks,

just as Harry usually does.

She picks up a lost marble.
It's blue, the color of cats' eyes.

Looking through the blue eye…

The windows are blue; the walls are blue.
The houses are blue; the sky is blue.
The world becomes a blue ocean world.

"I am a little fish, swimming in
the big, blue sea."
(Shau-yu means "little fish.")

Everything is blurry.

It's a blurry world.

But Shau-yu knows the way.

There's the shop, over there, near that pole.

"Hello shopkeeper. I would like to buy some eggs please, eggs for making fried rice. I am cooking fried rice and eggs for my family tonight."

"Here are your eggs, madam. And maybe your little girl, Shau-yu, would like some chewing gum?"

"Hmmm. I think she would."

The gum has lost its flavor. It's still good for blowing bubbles, though.

Pop!

It wakes Harry like magic.

Ding, dong.
"Hello! I've had such a busy day."

The Hsin Yi Picture Book Awards were created in 1987 to encourage local Taiwanese authors and illustrators to create high quality Chinese picture books for children.

On My Way to Buy Eggs won the award in 1997. The judges felt it would "make children feel there is endless happiness, humor and warmth in their everyday lives."

A note from the author:

Today when I looked out my window I saw a little girl carrying a bag of eggs. She was coming out of a traditional store. There are modern convenience stores nearby, but in the lanes there are still many traditional stores, quietly doing business. To me, traditional stores play a big part in my childhood memories.

When I was little I would hear my mother call from the kitchen, asking me to buy salt, soy sauce, or eggs from the traditional store. I would always see neighbors and friends in the store. It was a place that was much more than a shop for buying and selling.

It is nice to see that even though times have changed there are some things that remain the same.

A note from the publisher:

Traditional stores are little neighborhood stores, of the kind before supermarkets and convenience stores appeared. And, while there aren't quite so many of them anymore, they still exist in most neighborhoods in Taiwan. People can get almost anything they need there, from light bulbs to snacks, toilet paper to bug spray. They are combination drug stores, hardware stores, markets and marriage consultants (the shop owner!).